Disney · PIXAR

NSIDE OUT

JOY

by **Brittany Candau**
illustrated by **Jerrod Maruyama**

DISNEP PRESS
Los Angeles · New York

Hi, there!

I'm

I'm in charge
of being ... well ...
joyful!
And let me tell you,
there are a lot of things
to be happy about.

Like **dinos**

ROAR!!!

ROAR!!!

aurs!

And **sp**r**i**nkles on
cupcakes.

And
monkeys!

Ooh, and bouncy

balls!

You know what else is really great? Making goofy faces.

And twirling.
You just gotta

twirl
sometimes.

Sunshine
is my
absolute

favorite.

Ooh, but

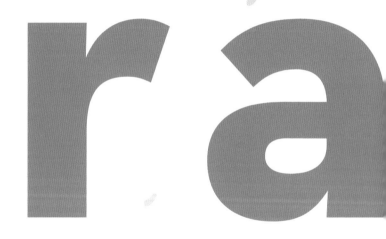

in

is my favorite, too!

You know what else is cool?

Shiny red bicycles!

Beautiful
SAN FRANCISCO

Greetings from...

And **new adventures** are the best!

But most of all, I've found that happiness is being with your friends and family!

Um, Joy?
I think you stepped
on my foot.